Born in Arbroath, Scotland, Joan spent her early childhood in Cambridgeshire. She began her working life as a secretary but ultimately fulfilled her ambition to become a primary school teacher. Her teaching career spanned over 30 years and took her from Bedford to West Sussex where she taught in four schools ultimately becoming a head teacher of a rural primary school. Joan experienced many changes during this time from no national curriculum and limited resources to Ofsted inspections, interactive whiteboards and a wonderful selection of fiction and non-fiction books. One thing which always remained constant was Joan's love of literature. Story time was always an important part of the day and an inspiration for cross-curriculum work inspiring drama and creative experiences. Joan now lives in a village in the South Downs of West Sussex and enjoys gardening, keeping bees, painting and writing.

POLAR BEAR, POLAR BEAR

JOAN KEIR BURNETT

AUSTIN MACAULEY PUBLISHERS™

LONDON • CAMBRIDGE • NEW YORK • SHARJAH

ISBN 9781398416130 (Paperback)
ISBN 9781398416147 (Hardback)
ISBN 9781398416161 (ePub e-book)
ISBN 9781398416154 (Audiobook)

www.austinmacauley.com

First Published (2021)
Austin Macauley Publishers Ltd
25 Canada Square
Canary Wharf
London
E14 5LQ

I dedicate this book to my children Matthew, James and Tom, and to my grandchildren Oliver, Charlie, Pippa, Harry, Tommy, Ed, Emilia and Max.

I also dedicate this book to the hundreds of children I have been lucky enough to teach over the years from Goldington Road First School, Bedford, Graffham Infant School, West Sussex, Westbourne C.P. School West Sussex, where I served as deputy head teacher, and at Compton & Up Marden CE Primary School also in West Sussex, where I served as head teacher.

A special dedication goes to art teacher Ian Patterson and youth leader Mike Harvey (Swavesey Village College) who encouraged me to pursue a teaching career.

A special thank you to David, who always encourages and supports me in everything I do.

Polar Bear, Polar Bear, what do you see?

I see my white furry mother looking at me and soft fluffy snow and icy cold sea.

6

Polar Bear, Polar Bear, what do you see?

I see snowflakes that flutter and tickle my nose
and icebergs that move with
the water that flows.

Polar Bear, Polar Bear, what do you hear?

I hear icy wind blowing as it touches my ear and
silence, just silence, when
nothing is near.

Polar Bear, Polar Bear, what do you hear?

I hear seals when they bark as they swim up for
air and whales as they splash
and dive with such flair.

Polar Bear, Polar Bear, what do you smell?

I smell freshly caught fish from the depths of the
sea which I enjoy for my
breakfast, supper and tea.

Polar Bear, Polar Bear, what do you smell?

I smell the air like my mother with head lifted
high and watch out for
strangers who may wander by.

Polar Bear, Polar Bear, what do you feel?

I feel the warmth from the sun as it shines its
bright light and watch as it
melts the ice with its might.

Polar Bear, Polar Bear, what do you feel?

I feel shivers and quivers from the cold wind that
blows and snowflakes that
melt as they touch my warm nose.

Polar Bear, Polar Bear, what have you learned?

I've learned that I live in a wonderful world of
ice and cold water, snow and
icebergs, seals, fish and whales
and beautiful birds.

Polar Bear, Polar Bear, what have you learned?

I've learned to listen to Mother and do what
she says so that I stay happy and
safe for the rest of my days.

Goodbye, Polar Bear, goodbye.